HOW'S THE WEATHER?

It's Windy!

Julie Richards

Smart Apple Media

This edition first published in 2005 in the United States of America by Smart Apple Media.

Smart Apple Media
1980 Lookout Drive
North Mankato
Minnesota 56003

Library of Congress Cataloging-in-Publication Data

Richards, Julie.
  It's windy! / by Julie Richards.
    p. cm. — (How's the weather?)
  Includes bibliographical references and index.
  Contents: How's the weather? — Wind — A windy day — Windy day gear —
  Where does wind come from? — Windy seasons — Built for wind — We need wind —
  Too much wind — Not enough wind — Dangerous winds — Wind science —
  Twisting winds — Windy sayings — Weather wonders — Try this!
  ISBN 1-58340-538-0 (alk. paper)
  1. Winds—Juvenile literature. [1. Winds.] I. Title.
  QC931.4.R53 2004
  551.51'8—dc22   2003070413
First Edition
9 8 7 6 5 4 3 2 1

First published in 2004 by
MACMILLAN EDUCATION AUSTRALIA PTY LTD
627 Chapel Street, South Yarra 3141

Associated companies and representatives throughout the world.

Copyright © Julie Richards 2004

Edited by Vanessa Lanaway
Page layout by Domenic Lauricella
Illustrations by Melissa Webb
Photo research by Legend Images

Printed in China

Acknowledgements
The author and the publisher are grateful to the following for permission to reproduce copyright material:

Cover photograph: boys flying kite, courtesy of Getty Images/Taxi.

Jean-Marc La Rocque/Auscape, p. 9; OSF/Auscape, pp. 15, 26; S. Wilby & C. Ciantar/Auscape, p. 27; Australian Picture Library/Corbis, pp. 21, 28; Getty Images/Image Bank, pp. 4, 11; Getty Images/Stone, p. 16; Getty Images/Taxi, pp. 1, 10, 14; Imageaddict, p. 6; Photodisc, pp. 5, 18, 19, 20, 23, 29; Photolibrary.com, p. 8; Reuters, p. 17; Terry Oakley/The Picture Source, pp. 7, 22, 25, 30.

While every care has been taken to trace and acknowledge copyright, the publisher tenders their apologies for any accidental infringement where copyright has proved untraceable. Where the attempt has been unsuccessful, the publisher welcomes information that would redress the situation.

Please note
At the time of printing, the Internet addresses appearing in this book were correct. Owing to the dynamic nature of the Internet, however, we cannot guarantee that all these addresses will remain correct.

Contents

How's the Weather?

Have you noticed how the weather always changes? You might see rain falling or hear thunder, feel warm sunshine or a cold wind blowing. Weather changes from day to day and **season** to season.

It can be hard to stand up on a windy day!

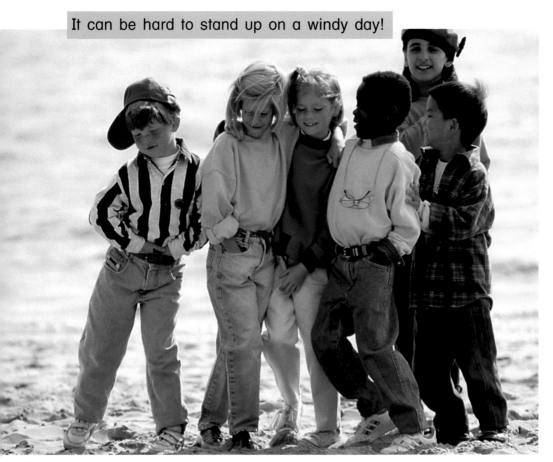

A strong wind is moving these palm trees.

The weather varies from place to place, too.
Some places are very windy. Dust, leaves, and
sometimes branches blow about everywhere.
Most places have both windy and still weather.
How's the weather where you live?

5

Wind

Wind is moving air. A breeze is gently moving air that only ruffles the leaves on trees. Strong winds, called gales, can blow things over. A sudden rush of wind is called a gust.

A gentle breeze is not strong enough to move this flag.

Wind can push the sea into giant waves.

Some large storms can bring great swirling
winds that destroy buildings and tear trees
from the ground. Other storms cause huge
waves out at sea.

A Windy Day

On a windy day, swirling dust can sting your eyes. You might hear the clatter of garbage being blown along the street. If the wind is very strong, you might find it difficult to stand up.

It can be difficult to walk in strong winds.

Strong winds can be dangerous for ships at sea.

Beside the sea on a windy day, you can watch boats bobbing on the waves. You might taste the salt spray blown from the water. Seabirds sometimes have trouble flying straight in the wind!

Windy Day Gear

What do you wear when it's windy? If it's cold, put on a coat, hat, and scarf to keep you warm. Then you can go outside and fly a kite.

Windy days are good for flying a kite.

Make sure you have warm clothes to wear on a windy day.

If it's raining too, you can put on a raincoat. You won't need an umbrella, though. If it's very windy, the wind will blow it inside out!

Where Does Wind Come From?

Wind is made by air that is heated by the sun.

When cool air and warm air move about we call it wind.

3 Warm air cools and sinks back to Earth.

2 The warm air rises.

1 The sun heats the ground and the air above it.

The ground in a shady forest will take much longer to warm up than a desert that has no shade. Deserts often have strong winds that push the sand into huge hills called dunes.

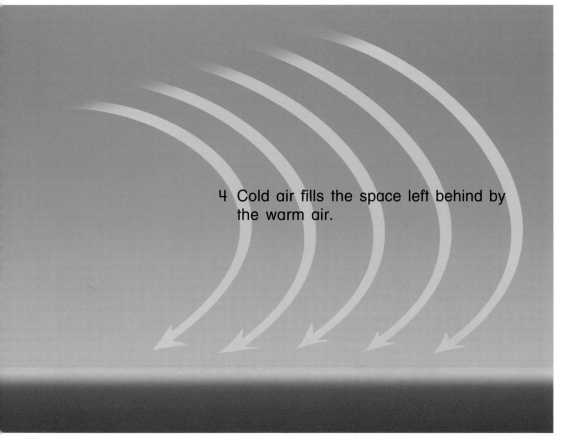

4 Cold air fills the space left behind by the warm air.

Windy Seasons

Winter and spring are often the windiest seasons. Winter can bring icy winds, which make you very cold. In summer, wind can cool you down after very hot weather. Fall winds spread plant seeds and blow dead leaves from the trees.

Dandelion seeds are scattered by the wind.

Monsoon winds bring heavy rain during the wet season.

Places that are warm all year have only two seasons—wet and dry. During the wet season, powerful winds called monsoons push gigantic rain clouds across the sky. Rain tumbles down almost all the time during monsoons.

Built for Wind

Wind can shake very tall buildings and make them sway. Some buildings have their outside walls strengthened. Others have a concrete block or water-filled tank inside the roof, which soaks up the movement.

This building has metal crosses to strengthen its outside walls.

This mobile home was blown over by strong winds.

Mobile homes are easily flipped or crushed by very strong winds. There are special shelters in places where fierce windstorms happen often. Mobile home owners can stay in them until the danger has passed.

17

We Need Wind

We need wind to spin the blades on wind turbines. Wind turbines use the wind to make some of our electricity, and pump water from **wells** for drinking. Wind also carries plant seeds to fresh soil, where they begin to grow.

Wind turbines use the wind to make electricity.

Sometimes, the wind is just a gentle breeze. Windsurfing, windskating, and yachting are exciting sports that need strong wind to help them move along.

Too Much Wind

Too much wind can lift roofs off buildings and push ships onto jagged rocks. Strong winds can carry burning leaves from wildfires. Wherever they drop, new fires can start.

Strong winds can flip small aircraft.

These plants have been flattened by strong winds.

Strong winds can flatten farmers' **crops** and shake fruit from orchard trees. If wind blows dry soil away, there may not be enough good soil left to plant next year's crops.

Dangerous Winds

Wind carries chemicals from factories, cars, and power stations into the air. The chemicals mix with clouds to make acid snow or acid rain. This eats into buildings and statues, and poisons forests, lakes, and rivers.

Wind can blow dirty air across a city.

Volcanoes shoot ash and smoke high into the air when they erupt.

The wind can also carry smoke and ash from an erupting volcano. Aircraft pilots must be very careful. Aircraft engines can become clogged with the ash and stop working. This could cause an aircraft to crash.

Forecasting Wind

Scientists who **forecast** weather are called meteorologists. They use computers and a **radiosonde** to collect information about the weather. This information is used to forecast weather.

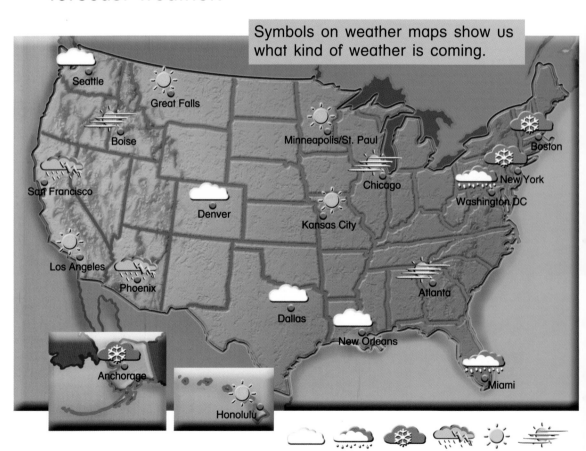

Symbols on weather maps show us what kind of weather is coming.

Seattle · Great Falls · Boise · San Francisco · Minneapolis/St. Paul · Chicago · Boston · New York · Washington DC · Denver · Kansas City · Los Angeles · Phoenix · Atlanta · Dallas · New Orleans · Miami · Anchorage · Honolulu

Clouds   Rain   Snow   Storms   Sun   Wind

Meteorologists measure wind speed with an **anemometer**. Wind spins cups on the anemometer. The faster the wind blows, the faster the cups spin. Meteorologists also use **radar** to tell them if the wind is likely to form a **tornado**.

Wind speed and direction is measured by an anemometer.

Twisting Winds

Twisting winds are very powerful. A tornado is a fiercely spinning wind that hangs from a thunderstorm cloud. It acts like a giant vacuum cleaner, sucking up everything in its path.

A tornado is the fastest wind on Earth.

Dust Devils

A dust devil is a twisting wind that always begins on the ground. Dust devils carry dust and sand, and sometimes leaves or bits of paper into the air.

Dust devils usually happen when the ground is very hot.

Windy Sayings

People use weather sayings and words to describe everyday things.

It's an ill wind that blows nobody any good.
People say this when they have a feeling something bad is about to happen.

I've had a windfall.
A windfall is when someone receives a treat they weren't expecting. This saying was first used when apples blew off trees, and people picked them up and kept them.

This is a windfall of apples.

Weather Wonders

Did you know?

⭐ The fastest wind gust ever recorded was on top of Mount Washington, United States of America, in 1934. It was as fast as a Formula One racing car.

⭐ A tornado once sucked up a herd of cows from a field. The cows were later found sitting on top of a barn roof. Once, frogs were sucked into a tornado and frozen inside hailstones. When the hailstones melted on the ground, the frogs hopped away!

⭐ The windiest place on Earth is Antarctica. The wind blows so hard that it can knock people over and blow them away.

Try This!

Ask a parent or teacher for help.

Moving air

⭐ Draw a spiral on a sheet of stiff paper.

⭐ Cut out the spiral by starting at the outside of the paper and cutting round and round until you reach the center.

⭐ Make a hole in the center of the spiral. Thread a piece of cotton or wool through it and tie a knot in the end.

⭐ Hold the spiral over something warm, such as a lamp that has been on for a while. What happens to the spiral?

The warm air rising from the lamp makes the spiral start to twirl.

Glossary

anemometer	an instrument for measuring wind speed and direction
crops	plants grown for food
forecast	to know what kind of weather is coming
radar	a way of looking at faraway objects
radiosonde	a number of instruments fixed to a special balloon, used to collect information about weather
season	a part of the year that has its own kind of weather
tornado	a fiercely spinning wind
wells	holes dug in the ground to find water

Index

Weather on the Web

Here are some Web sites that you might like to look at:
http://www.ucar.edu/40th/webweather
http://www.fema.gov/kids/hurr.htm
http://www.education.noaa.gov/sweather.html